THE KISS THAT MISSED
by David Melling

British Library Cataloguing in Publication Data
A catalogue record of this book is available from
the British Library.
ISBN: 0 340 911476

Copyright © David Melling 2002

The right of David Melling to be identified as
the author and illustrator of this Work has been asserted
by him in accordance with the Copyright, Designs and
Patents Act 1988.

First edition published 2002
This mini hardback edition published 2006
10 9 8 7 6 5 4 3 2 1

Published by Hodder Children's Books
a division of Hodder Headline Limited
338 Euston Road London NW1 3BH

Printed in China

THE KISS
THAT MISSED

Written and illustrated by

DAVID MELLING

Hodder
Children's
Books

A division of Hodder Headline Limited

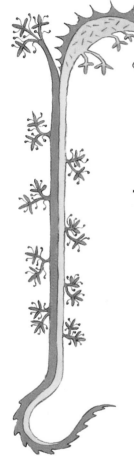

ONCE UPON A
Tuesday the king was
in a hurry as usual.
'Goodnight,' he said,
and blew his son a
royal kiss.

It missed.

The young prince watched it rattle around the room,
then bounce out of the window and into the night.

The prince told the queen.

The queen told the king
and the king had a quick
word with his loyal knight.

'Follow that kiss!'
he squawked.

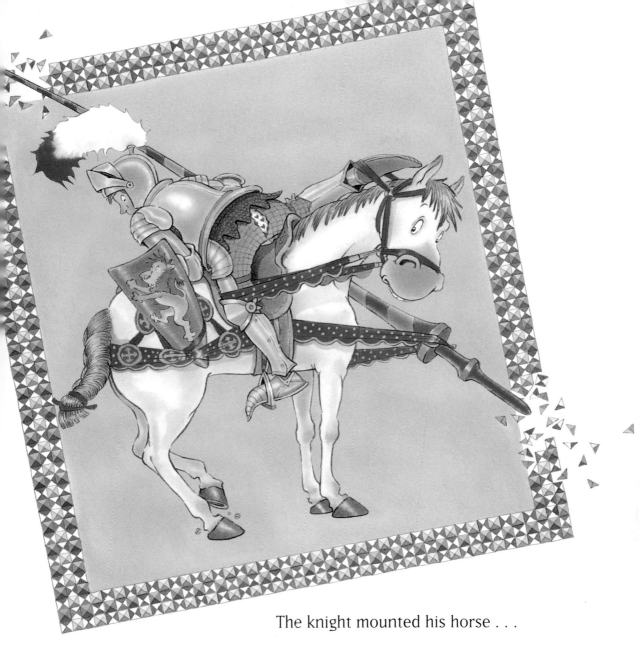

The knight mounted his horse . . .

. . . eventually . . .

and galloped off in hot pursuit until
they came to the wild wood.

Wild creatures with wild eyes,
too much hair and very bad manners
lived here.

It was dark,
It was smelly,
It was . . .

. . . snowing.

They were not alone.

There were bears with long claws
and growly roars, swooping owls
of all shapes and sizes . . .

. . . and a pack of hungry wolves
with dribbly mouths.

'EEK!'
squeaked the knight.
And then, suddenly . . .

... with a sparkle the royal kiss came floating by

and, in turn, said goodnight to everyone.

Bears stopped being growly.
Owls stopped being swoopy.
Wolves stopped being dribbly.
And before you could say 'big, hairy toes'
they all settled down for a good night's sleep.

The wrinkly old
tree trunk twitched . . .

So, the knight and his
faithful horse sat down
on a wrinkly old tree
trunk to rest.

. . . and slowly rose
into the air . . .

. . . above the woods and into the clouds.

At last they found themselves staring into a pair of giant nostrils.

A dragon with 'this lot would be nice for breakfast' eyes leered greedily at them.

Suddenly . . . .

. . . with a sparkle the royal kiss came floating by and flew right up the dragon's nose.

He sat up, sniffed and blinked.

Slowly, he opened his mouth,
took a deep breath and . . .

. . . sneezed!

'Hang on!' he said, as they tumbled through the trees.
'Come back!' he puffed, as he lumbered after them.

'I want to pick you up and . . .'

'. . . kiss you goodnight.'

Slowly they all made their way back to the castle.

That night the prince was happy,

the queen was happy,

and the king promised to stop
always being in a hurry.

He made sure everyone was comfortable and
slowly read them a bedtime story
from beginning to end . . .

. . . almost.